Finnigan's Bliss

Charlotte Jackson ♡

Charlotte
Jackson
♡

"Your light will shine, your clouds will part,
With a peaceful mind and a loving heart."

Finnigan was a little goat that lived
in a cozy barn, on a gentle farm.

Every morning, Finnigan began
his day the very same way. He'd
wake up, eager for adventure, and
his loving mother would tell him,
"Finnigan, delight in all the little
gifts that come your way, for they
will fill your day with bliss."

Then he'd cheerfully amble outside to soak
in the warmth of the rising sun.

Next, he'd romp out to the meadow and rub the little buds of his little horns against his favourite post, where an old fence once stood. He'd cherish the lumpy, bumpy wood that reached his little itchy spots like nothing else could do!

Scritchity-scratchity! Scritchity-scratchity!
his little head nodded with gratification.

Ahhh, sighed Finnigan. *This is bliss.*

When his little legs felt frisky with
life, he'd prance through the field
and rollick amongst the flowers.
He'd revel in the long, flowing grass
that tickled his little belly.

Hippity-hoppity! Hippity-hoppity!
his little hooves bounced with exhilaration.

Ahhh, sighed Finnigan. *This is bliss.*

When his little tummy felt rumbly
with hunger, he'd lounge in the
shade of a tree and nibble on the
tender, green alfalfa. He'd relish
the delicious flavour that tasted
sweet on his little tongue.

Crunchity-munchity! Crunchity-munchity!
his little mouth savoured with satisfaction.

Ahhh, sighed Finnigan. *This is bliss.*

When his little eyelids felt
heavy with sleep, he'd curl
up next to his loving mother
and drift into dreams. He'd
bask in the soothing sound
of the chicks' melodies
that hushed and lulled
his whole little body.

Cheepity-peepity! Cheepity-peepity!
his little ears listened with appreciation.

Ahhh, sighed Finnigan. *This is bliss.*

One morning, Finnigan began his day the very same way. He woke up, eager for adventure, and his loving mother reminded him, "Finnigan, delight in all the little gifts that come your way, for they will fill your day with bliss."

Then he cheerfully ambled outside to soak
in the warmth of the rising sun. But this
day was not the same as every other.

Misty rain drizzled from the somber, grey sky.
Damp air chilled his little nose. Still, he decided to
romp out to the meadow and rub the little buds of
his little horns against his lumpy, bumpy post.

But something else had changed overnight.

"Where is my scratching post?"
Finnigan asked himself, so confused.

Frantically, he searched high and low
to find that the wind had carelessly
tossed it into a soggy, sloppy puddle!

As he stared at the wood lying in muck, the rain began to pour down in buckets, seemingly unconcerned for little Finnigan, drenched and miserable.

Suddenly, his
mind couldn't
think,

and his little
body trembled.

He didn't know
what to do!

So he kicked and
he reared and he
bleated mournfully!

BAAA-WAAA!
BAAAA-WAAAA!
his little voice wailed
with frustration.

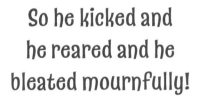

OH NO! THIS IS TERRIBLE!
BAAAA-WAAAA!!
he bleated again.

Then in the midst of the pelting rain, he thought he
heard a small voice whisper, "Just breathe."

"What did you say?" Finnigan looked around, bewildered.

"You will feel better if you take a breath,"
the mysterious voice replied.

"What do you mean? I AM breathing!"
Finnigan insisted.

"Take a slow, dee-eep breath."

**"WHO are you? WHERE are you?
PLEASE let me see you!"** Finnigan
pleaded, more befuddled than ever.

"I am Samuel. Look down here."

"Oh, there you are.
Are you hurt Samuel?"

"No, I am fine. But while I was lounging in this lovely puddle of muck, this large log fell and trapped me, so I cannot return to my home in the creek."

Despite his deep despair, Finnigan
stopped kicking and rearing and bleating,
and he lifted his beloved and battered
scratching post off the small frog.

"Thank you for your compassion," Samuel croaked with relief. "Now, do as I do and take a slow, deep breath. Fill your little belly with air the way I fill my throat when I croak."

Finnigan watched Samuel, and he filled his little belly with the pleasant aroma of wet hay.

"That's it! Now take another," encouraged Samuel.

Finnigan took another slow, deep breath.
And his mind cleared.
So he took another slow, deep breath.
And his little body settled.

He took a few more slow, deep breaths with Samuel.
He paid attention to the fresh air that
flowed in and out of his little chest.

Sniffity-snuffity...sni-iffity-snu-uffity...
his little nose inhaled and exhaled with relaxation.

Ahhh, sighed Finnigan. *Now I feel...calm.*

"Thank you Samuel. My name is Finnigan.
Please let me help you up onto my back,
and I'll gladly take you home."

"I accept your considerate offer,"
replied the small frog.

As the little goat plodded along, the rain drummed persistently on their backs. Finnigan was no longer distressed, but his heart still felt heavy.

"I surely cannot find any little gifts to delight in today," he complained with sorrow.

Samuel, on the other hand,
was soaked with rain
and beamed with joy!

"But isn't this rain wonderful?"
he happily remarked.

"I don't think so," Finnigan mumbled.
"It makes me feel sad. I am cold and
wet, and the sky is so dreary."

Samuel listened thoughtfully then explained, "That may be true, but when things seem bleak, there is always a bright side, even if it is hard to see. This gloomy day brings the rain that feeds the grass, the flowers, and the trees and fills the creek with clean water."

"Yes, but my lumpy, bumpy post is lying in a soggy, sloppy puddle," Finnigan lamented.

Samuel nodded, "I understand. Indeed you have had some misfortune. But that moment has passed, so let it go. And believe that in time, things will turn out just fine."

Finnigan pondered Samuel's wise
words, and when they arrived
at the creek, he was weary and
waterlogged, yet warm inside.

"It was so nice to meet you Samuel. I feel much better. Now I'll be on my way back home."

But before he left, he gazed at the sprinkling raindrops that entranced his little eyes.

Pittery-pattery! Pittery-pattery!
his heart lightened with admiration.

Ahhh, sighed Finnigan. *This is bliss.*

"Won't you stay and play?"
asked Samuel.

"No, I really shouldn't," Finnigan
thought. He'd had such a challenging
morning, and all he wanted
was to curl up on his soft bed
of straw and take a nap!

Then Samuel smiled with
such kindness, that Finnigan
suddenly realized...the delightful
little gift that he couldn't find
had been there all along.

"Well, maybe for a little while," Finnigan decided.

And what a **fine** decision that **turned out** to be.

Spishity-splashity! Splishity-splashity!
the new-found friends frolicked with elation.

As they played the clouds parted, and the sun's shimmering rays shone through, revealing an exquisite little gift.

Finnigan and Samuel sat and marveled at the magical splendor that captured their hearts.

In that moment of stillness and silence,
their minds soared with inspiration.

Aaaahhhhh, they both sighed.
This...is...bliss.

Tellwell Talent
www.tellwell.ca

ISBN
978-1-77370-868-3 (Hardcover)
978-1-77370-867-6 (Paperback)

CPSIA information can be obtained
at www.ICGtesting.com
Printed in the USA
LVHW071948071118
596307LV00014B/136/P